Lee Aucoin, *Creative Director*
Jamey Acosta, *Senior Editor*
Heidi Fiedler, *Editor*
Produced and designed by
Denise Ryan & Associates
Illustration © Mike Gordon
Rachelle Cracchiolo, *Publisher*

Teacher Created Materials
5301 Oceanus Drive
Huntington Beach, CA 92 649-1030
http://www.tcmpub.com
Paperback: ISBN: 978-1-4333-5606-3
Library Binding: ISBN: 978-1-4807-1728-2

Written by
Michael McMahon

Illustrated by
Mike Gordon

Contents

GOODBYE
Cars
To GIANT Tortoises
ICE CREAM
This way
COOL DRINKS
Lemurs
Bear
Wrong way!
To the Emu run
ZOO

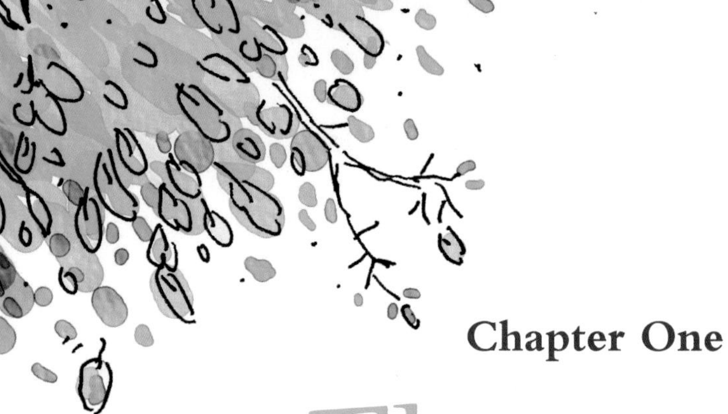

Chapter One

The Zoo Crew

So you want to be a zookeeper? Marvelous! We can help you become a zookeeper extraordinaire. (That means you will be an out-of-the-ordinary zookeeper.) Zookeepers can work anywhere in the world. (That means you could work in zoos in Melbourne, Moscow, Basel, or Berlin!)

You can join our zoo crew today! You can help feed the animals and clean their pens. You will have plenty of hands-on action with some of our wonderful animals. All you need to do is dress up for the occasion.

So let's start your zoo-keeping lessons with Aldabra tortoises. You will be the envy of all your friends. You can help with our giant tortoise display. First, you need to know a few things before you tiptoe into their pen.

Sometimes, the tortoises think they are Olympic gymnasts. They rise up on their hind legs to eat low-hanging tree branches for lunch. Make sure you aren't under the trees when the tortoises come down to Earth. There won't be much of you left if you are! You may also like to know tortoises love to eat squashed people.

Do you think tortoises are slow and cautious? Usually, they are. But giant tortoises are very, very strong. They can ram through fences and doors. It's scary to watch! Don't stand between an Aldabra tortoise and the gate! You never know when one might want to go home to his mom.

Yes, tortoises are dangerous. Sadly, an anti-tortoise spray, found at all good drugstores, won't work. It won't repel flies or mosquitoes, either. And they're hungry!

Chapter Two

Lemur Land

Let's meet the lemurs. They have a haunting stare—when they're awake. Now, would you believe lemurs don't usually live in the Central Park Zoo? Most lemurs live in Madagascar. But we do have a troop here, so you will be able meet them today.

Lemurs sleep during the day. Listen to them snoring away! It's always a good idea to wear your black-and-white hard hat. If a lemur falls on you, he will think you are a large, two-legged, black-and-white lemur. When you are near sleeping lemurs, protect yourself by singing lullabies. "Rock-a-bye, Baby" will keep them asleep all day!

Lemurs like to eat coconuts, tamarinds, pineapples, and mangoes. And they love a cup of strong black coffee when they wake up. We always have pure Madagascar coffee ready for them at 8:00 PM. They prefer to drink from fine china. We have imported some lovely cups from France. Nothing is too good for our lemurs!

All good zookeepers know the names of their animals. So you will need to learn the lemurs' names. We will give you a memory test tomorrow morning when they have gone back to sleep. We have Lee, Lan, Li, Lars, and Leif. Good luck!

Chapter Three

Emu Run

Now, it's time to meet our emus. Emus are very large birds. They come from Australia. Emus have lived there for ages. Their ancestors even roamed the land when dinosaurs lived.

Our emus are training for the Emu Speed Marathon. You can train with the birds. But when running thirty miles per hour, they can be very hard to catch. Once again, good luck!

It's a good idea to start all your training runs in the lane marked *Humans*. Emus have very good eyesight. But they can't read very well. You'll be safe in the human lane. As long as you don't look like a dingo, the emus won't jump over you or kick you in the shins.

Each of your strides will need to cover at least nine feet. That's if you want to keep up with the mob. We've found that it's best to start running at least twelve hours before the emus do. That means you will be out in front for at least a minute.

Make sure you keep your candy safe. Please don't take it with you when you are running on the track. Emus usually like to eat flowers, berries, and insects. But they will eat anything they can find! They have been known to eat stones, dirt, and tin cans. Your candy is much more colorful than stones and dirt. Emus would love it!

After your run, you might like to join the emus in the pool. All you need to do is roll on your back. Then, kick your legs in the air. The emus will show you how! Emus can swim, but they prefer to do their leg exercises above the water.

WARNING: Avoid painting your toenails. The emus might nibble them!

POOL

Chapter Four

The Zookeeper Test

A zookeeper test? Yes, there always has to be a test! It doesn't matter if you are at school or at the zoo. We have a test for you. It's to show you can be a zookeeper extraordinaire.

What is the name of the chief tortoise?

You didn't know there was a chief tortoise? We must have forgotten to tell you! Do you think the chief tortoise is called Aldrick, which means "wise old ruler," or Amo, which means "little eagle"?

Answer: Who cares?

Where do Aldabra tortoises come from?

Oh, we didn't tell you that either? Maybe you can figure it out. Are they from the Aldabra Islands in the Indian Ocean or Finland?

Answer: Whoops! Too easy!

What do lemurs like to drink?

Now, we're sure you know the answer to this one! Do lemurs like to drink pure Madagascar coffee, lime smoothies, or parsley milkshakes?
Answer: Well, it's one of the above!

What are the names of the lemurs?

Are they Rae, Rane, Ralph, Raj, and Rad?

Answer: Nope. Well done. You're on your way to becoming a zookeeper extraordinaire!

Michael McMahon lives in Melbourne, Australia. One day he went to the Werribee Open Range Zoo to watch the zookeepers at work. As soon as he saw what fun they had, he wanted to be a zookeeper, too. Then, he changed his mind and decided he would write about how to become one. Better safe than sorry!

Mike Gordon was born in England but now lives in Santa Barbara, California. Since living in California, he's been so busy drawing hundreds of illustrations that he rarely has time to enjoy the sunshine!